SOLDIER'S SYMPHONY

EMMA BRAY

CHAPTER 1

Harper

"OH, come on, Harper! You have to go with us!"

Meg is looking up at me with her big blue eyes. She widens them so they look like puppy dog eyes and pouts as she begs. "It'll be so much fun! I promise you. All you ever do is work. You need to get out and live a little."

I sigh. Meg's got me there. Ever since my dad died, all I've done is work. Of course, I do it to make ends meet, but I've also taken on extra shifts—as many as I can to keep busy.

My dad left me the little bungalow where I grew up. He was smart enough to make sure the house was completely paid off long ago, so it's not like I have a mortgage or rent to worry about. I just have to pay my electric bill and taxes and buy my food and necessities.

Most of what I'm earning now goes into a small savings account. I don't know what I'm saving up for. My dreams died the day my dad did. I just don't have the passion for anything I used to anymore.

I finish wiping down my table while Meg continues to flutter around me like a butterfly. "All the other waitresses are going," she adds. "Molly and Mary will be there. And even Chrissy."

I try not to wrinkle up my nose at the mention of Chrissy, though I can tell by Meg's face that she's not exactly thrilled Chrissy will be there either.

Chrissy acts like she's better than the rest of us and makes it clear every time she steps through the doors that she doesn't need this job. She's just doing it to make extra money before she goes to college.

Besides Chrissy, I get along well with all of my co-workers, especially Meg, who barnacled herself onto me the moment I walked in the door. She decided I needed a friend and applied herself generously to that role.

Growing up as an only child, I didn't have a lot of friends. It was always just my dad and me. I'm a little on the quiet side. I'm not exactly shy, but I never saw the need to be the life of the party. I was the kind of girl who could talk to my classmates and get along well with all of them. I was pretty well-liked, but I wasn't particularly close to anyone.

But none of that matters now that we're all grown up. I'm waiting tables here at the diner, and only God knows what the rest of them are doing. If I had to bet, I would guess most of them are in college now. Many of my classmates were trust fund babies.

I honestly don't know how my dad could afford to send me to private school, but he insisted that I get a good education in a safe environment.

My heart wrenches at the thought of him. It's been two years, yet I still miss him like it was yesterday. He was my best friend.

I never knew my mother. She died giving birth to me, but my father never held that against me—even when I held it against myself. He told me that I was her pride and joy when she was pregnant and that she wouldn't have regretted her sacrifice. Dad also assured me that she'd be so proud of the woman I'd become.

Meg's face falls as if she can tell the turn my thoughts have taken. Meg is a good friend. She's been here for me through it all.

The day I got the phone call that my dad was in a

bad car crash, she was the one who held me while I cried. She knows firsthand what I've been through. She was there to wrap her arms around me when I needed someone to cry on, and I'll forever be grateful to her for that.

I'm not into all this social stuff, though. After a long day at work, I like to go home and relax by myself with a good book or a movie, but I know my friend means well. She just worries about me.

That's why I hear myself agreeing. "Sure, Meg. Count me in."

"Sweet!" she squeals as she flutters off to get back to work.

I smile to myself. Maybe it will be good for me to get out for a night with the girls.

———

The girls don't take me to a rambunctious club, and for that, I'm thankful. I'm so not into the club scene. Instead, we hit up a local bar where the vibe is good, and there's no pressure to dance and gyrate all over one another like there is at a club.

We're all dressed pretty casually in skirts and tank tops, but nothing outrageous.

I instantly relax as we drink a few flirty cocktails

and the girls' chatter. They talk about some of our usual customers, and Meg makes this hilarious impression of one of our grumpiest regulars that has us all laughing.

I grip my stomach with deep belly laughs—the kind that I haven't experienced in years. It's the kind of laugh that makes your stomach hurt but in a good way. I wipe the tears from my eyes. Meg was right. This feels good. Yes, I still miss my dad, but I know he wouldn't want me to grieve for him forever. He would want me to have friends and start living again.

So, I vow to myself that's what I'm going to do.

We're a couple of drinks in when people start going up on the stage for to sing karaoke. Unsurprisingly, Chrissy is the first one in our group to volunteer. We all giggle and clap supportively. She's not as good a singer as she thinks she is, but she's not horrible, either. She's just a little over the top.

"Okay, now it's your turn, Harper." Meg turns her big blue eyes on me.

"Oh, no." I shake my head, my palms sweating at the thought of getting on the stage in front of a bunch of people—even if they are people I don't know.

"Yes, you have to!" Molly and Mary agree. "We'll go after you, but you go next."

"No, girls, I really don't want to," I protest, but Meg

is already plucking my drink from my fingers and pulling me to stand.

"Harper, you're an amazing singer. You'll do great!" she tells me.

I give her a pleading look.

Yes, Meg has heard me sing. I used to love singing, but it's something I haven't done much of since my father died. That was kind of *our* thing. Dad played the guitar while I sang along with him. He loved to hear me sing. At one time, I even dreamed of going to music school and studying the vocal arts, but I gave all that up when Dad died. Just like I've pretty much given up singing.

Something I know my dad wouldn't want. He'd be so sad knowing I've stopped singing, and that thought cements my decision.

Meg continues to pull on my arm, and I finally concede. What the hell? So far, all of Meg's suggestions—like the one that I come out tonight—have turned out well. And I also vowed that I was going to let loose and live a little, so I'm just gonna go for it. Who cares if I bomb it, right? Everyone in this place is tipsy, and a lot of the people who've gotten up haven't been good singers. Karaoke is all in good fun anyway. It's not like we're seriously out to impress anyone.

"Okay, what are you going to sing, little lady?" the DJ manning the karaoke asks me with a wink.

I glance over at Meg. I don't have the first clue what to choose, but in true Meg fashion, she's ready to volunteer something.

I know the song she suggests, so I shrug at the DJ and go with it. It's not one of the campy, cheesy, upbeat songs, but it's not a slow song either. It's more of a rock-pop ballad—one that I remember singing a lot with my dad while he played the electric guitar.

I let the music wash over me. I haven't sung much in the past couple of years, but I still love to listen to music, losing myself in the chords and melodies.

I close my eyes when the song reaches the opening stanza. It's my cue to sing, so I take a deep breath, open my mouth, and let loose.

I get lost in the lyrics, lost in the melody. I'm singing from the bottom of my heart, remembering my father. This is like a cleansing, a revelation, as I silently dedicate this song to him.

I get so caught up in my song that I forget where I am. When I open my eyes, the bar is so silent you can hear a pin drop. My face immediately flushes.

Oh, my God, I must have been horrible.

Suddenly, everyone erupts into applause, standing to their feet like they're at an opera or something.

People are hooting and hollering and cheering, and my face flushes even deeper.

I nod my head in a humble bow and leave the stage. When I walk back over to the table where the girls are sitting, Molly and Mary are typing furiously on their phones.

I glance over their shoulders as I pass by them and gasp when I see what they're up to. "Oh my god, you guys! You *cannot* post that!"

They took a video of me singing, and they're posting it online.

"Too late!" Molly chirps up at me as her finger presses the send button.

"Yeah, too late for me too!" Mary says with a huge grin.

I cover my face with my hands. I don't want to be all over the internet. I'm not good enough for all that.

"What's wrong?" Meg asks me. "You were freaking amazing!"

"No, I'm so out of practice!" I groan. "I didn't know you guys were taking a video!" I shoot them all a distressed glance.

"Babe, we weren't the only ones," Molly notes as she jerks her head toward the rest of the room where other people are on their phones.

My cheeks flame, and I catch Chrissy out of the

corner of my eye. She's glaring at me with her arms crossed, no doubt pissed off that I've stolen her thunder. Great. All I need is for her to be pissed off at me and give me more attitude than she already does at work. I was hoping that tonight would bridge the gap between us, and I think it did until my performance right after hers. I should have known better.

A few people come over to say hi to us and gush about my performance, and I sit there blushing like the idiot I am, feeling awkward. I've never been one for the spotlight, but I have to admit this feels good. It feels good to sing again and to hear that people enjoyed it.

When I finally go home, I have a smile on my face. For the first time in two years, I'm not crying as I fall asleep.

CHAPTER 2

Erik

I WORK my way through my business emails as I do every morning while the news plays in the background. Taking a sip of my black coffee, I scowl at my computer screen. Fucking Donovan. It's always something with him. I type out a quick reply before I hit "send."

I scoff when I see that Morta has made yet another bid for one of my compositions. He may as well give it up. I'll never sell my work to anyone.

My music is my life. It's personal. It's not for public use. He should consider himself lucky that I fund his little musical theater.

I realize that I'm a bit backward. Most composers want the world to hear their work and love it, but I'm just the opposite. I hoard my compositions close to my chest like a dragon hoards treasure. I'm greedy. I don't want to share them with anyone. I think part of the reason is I know that no one else will be able to do my pieces justice.

I take another sip of my brew before something on the television catches my eye. I don't know why I turn the news on every morning. I rarely watch it, but now and then, a clip will catch my attention.

But nothing has ever caught my attention like this.

There's a girl on the screen. She has a thin build and long chocolate curls that flow down to her waist. They frame her face, making her look cherubic, like something from one of those classical paintings.

Her eyes are closed, her dark lashes laying on her creamy-white cheeks. She's wearing a fluttery little black skirt and a sky-blue tank top that shows just a hint of skin between the hem of her shirt and the band of the skirt.

It's not the clothing that gets my attention, though. She's not scantily dressed, and while she's beautiful—the most beautiful little angel I've ever seen—it's not that either.

No, what gets my attention is the crystal pure

sound pouring from her pink lips. She has perfect pitch, her voice smooth and sweet. I've never heard anything like it in all my thirty-one years. Her voice is purity itself. I can't tear my eyes from her.

She's innocence personified, and that voice...

I'm suddenly burning to know everything about her. Who is she?

As if the news anchor hears my unspoken question, she answers, "That's Harper Young, ladies and gentleman, the waitress who's singing went viral last night."

She goes on to tell the story of how she and her friends were hanging out at this bar when Harper got up to do a karaoke number. Her friends filmed her and put her on the internet, and now she's become an overnight sensation.

"Harper." I taste the syllables on my lips. Sweet Jesus, her name tastes like honey. I speak it again, claiming it as mine.

Something inside me clicks. I've never wanted anyone to perform my compositions, but I'm suddenly dying to hear my music on her lips. It's crystal clear, like I've had an epiphany. It's her. She's who I've been waiting for. This marvelous, wonderful girl. This little angel sent down from heaven.

I pause the scene and rewind it to play back the

clip. I can't tear my eyes from her as I watch the emotion flood across her face and pour out into her voice. Even though she has her eyes closed, she puts more emotion into that one song than the most practiced of musicians.

My eyes rove over her from head to toe, desire coursing through my veins. I'm aroused for the first time in years. Well, I'm no monk. I've been taking care of my needs myself for a while now, but it's been a long time since any female has elicited such a reaction.

I jump from my desk, excitement coursing through my veins. I feel like I'll die if I don't get to her soon. I don't know what my plan is, but I take off toward my library door. I stop when my hand touches the doorknob, glancing to my right. My gaze is drawn there unbidden.

There's a mirror hanging in the corner of the room. I hate mirrors. I *hate* the fucking things, but I left this one up because it was my mother's. However, I put it in the most obscure location so I don't have to look at myself.

I look now and scoff as I raise my hand to my scarred visage. I trail my fingers over the mangled flesh on the right side of my face. Fortunately, my injury doesn't cause me much pain, but it scarred up the right half of my face, making me look like a monster.

I force myself to gaze upon my scarred face, my jaw hardening as reality comes crashing down upon me once again. I'm a monster now. I'm not the good-looking man I once was, the man who could saunter up to any female and ask her out with complete confidence.

I drop my hand from the doorknob and hunch my shoulders as I turn back toward my desk, dejected.

There's a reason I keep myself sequestered away from the rest of society. The mirror starkly reminds me of that fact. I don't know what came over me that I momentarily forgot.

My eyes flick back up to the screen where Harper's beautiful face is displayed. Yes, I do. This little song-bird with the voice and face of an angel. She's what came over me. I want her so bad it's a physical ache. My chest tightens, and I pull in panting breaths.

It can never be, I remind myself. She's beautiful and whole, whereas I'm half the man I used to be. She wouldn't give a poor sap like me the time of day.

I ball my hands into fists and lean on my desk, my jaw clenched so tightly I'm surprised I don't break the fucker. The hopelessness of my situation crashes over me until I roar in fury and swipe everything from my desk, knocking my laptop and everything onto the floor to shatter.

Nostrils flared, I grapple for control, my chest heaving like the beast I am. Shame washes over me at losing control like this. I'm no longer fit for polite society. This just proves it. I'm not worthy of an angel like her.

I look back at the screen, my heart breaking into a thousand pieces as I rewind the clip and watch it over and over and over again, torturing myself with the purity that I can never have.

I spend the next few days finding out everything about Harper Young. I have the best private investigator money can buy pull her file, and I study everything contained within it. I study her harder than I studied any course in college. She's twenty-one and waiting tables at a hole-in-the-wall diner—such a waste for a girl with her kind of talent.

I rewatch the clip of her singing like a man possessed. Her voice is ingrained in my head forever. I hear it when I sleep. I see her image every time I close my eyes. She's there all around me.

My world is irrevocably changed, and nothing will ever be the same again.

I have my man watch her all day while she's at

work. Everywhere she goes, I have him following her and sending me a live feed of what's going on. It's obsessive and crazy and over the top, but I don't give a damn.

Maybe I can't approach her on my own, but I'll make damn sure I keep my eyes on her. I can't explain it, but I have this insane need to know where she is at all times. I need to watch over her even though she has no clue I exist.

Her father passed away a couple of years ago, so she's all alone in this world. Anything could have happened to her in those years before I knew of her, but I vow that nothing will now because she has me silently watching over her, protecting her.

She'll never be alone again. Whether she knows it or not, I'll always be there in the shadows, her silent benefactor making sure she has anything she needs. My heart clenches painfully at the knowledge that's all I can ever be.

It's not about sex, although I'd be lying if I said I'm not dying to sheath myself in her heat. No, it's more than that. My arms ache to hold her, stroke her like a little kitten. Talk to her and climb inside her mind to hear every thought in her beautiful head. Make all her dreams come true.

I certainly have the means to. I have all this money

and no one to spend it on. What's the point in all of this if I have to do it alone? But I'm no longer alone because now I have a reason for living. I have Harper. I can take care of her, even if from afar.

I content myself with that until I turn on the TV one morning and see that Morta is on the morning news putting out a public offer for Harper to come work for him.

I drop my coffee cup, the hot beverage spilling onto my shirt and pants. It scalds me, but I barely feel the burn. My vision is blurring as panic seizes my chest.

There is no way in hell I'm going to let her work for another composer. I don't think I can bear for her to sing another man's compositions. The only songs she should be singing are mine.

I square my jaw with resolve.

When Harper sings, she's going to sing only for *me*.

CHAPTER 3

Harper

"HARPER, there's some guy at table nine who's insisting you wait on him."

I let out an exasperated breath and fight not to roll my eyes. I could strangle Meg, Molly, and Mary for posting that video. Of course, they weren't the only ones who posted the video of me singing. Plenty of the other people did, too. I should throttle them for talking me into going up there to do karaoke because tons of random strangers are now coming into the diner and specifically requesting me as their waitress.

They just want to get a picture of the girl on TV. It has nothing to do with my talent because while I think

I'm a decent singer, I'm far from the best. I've never had any musical training. Not professionally, anyway.

And I hate all of this spotlight. A video gets a ton of hits for whatever reason, the news reporters go on about it, and your life is completely turned upside down. I can't wait until the next big thing goes viral and I'm quietly forgotten so I can dissolve into the background again.

"Thanks, Meg." I grab my pen and paper and head over to the specified table. I try to give the man my biggest smile to hide my irritation. "Can I take your order?"

The gentleman in question is unremarkable. He's an older man with graying hair, but he's wearing a suit, which seems out of place at this hole-in-the-wall diner. He looks more like he belongs on Park Avenue.

"Hello, Harper. I'm Mr. Jenkins."

I don't even blink at him knowing my name. So many random strangers know my name now. I just smile at him and wait for him to place his order.

"Please have a seat, Harper," he says instead. "I was hoping we could talk."

"I'm on the job right now, sir," I politely decline.

"This will only take a minute, I assure you." He smiles at me kindly and motions for me to sit across from him.

"I really can't—" I begin, but he interrupts me.

"Please, Miss Young. I promise I won't waste your time."

I glance around, checking for the manager. When I don't see him anywhere, I slide into the booth across from the stranger. What can it hurt to sit for a minute and hear what he has to say? I'm not getting any creepy vibes from him, and now I'm curious.

He clears his throat before he begins. "I've been sent here with a proposition for you from my boss, Erik Duvall."

He pauses and looks at me expectantly.

I stare at him blankly.

He blinks and looks a bit taken aback. Should I recognize the name of his employer?

"Okay," I speak slowly.

Mr. Jenkins lets out a chuckle before he adds, "He's the most prominent composer in the city. He saw your video, and he wants to train you."

My mouth falls open at that. "What do you mean?" I ask warily.

"He wants to train you musically," Jenkins clarifies. "He thinks you have potential. He wants you to perform his compositions."

He's quiet again and levels me with a look like I

should understand how monumental this is, but I don't. I shake my head and shrug apologetically.

Jenkins chuckles again, leaning forward conspiratorially as if he's about to impart a great secret. "Miss Young, I don't think you understand the significance of this offer. Mr. Duvall is very protective of his compositions. He won't sell them. He's never let anyone perform them, yet he wants *you* to perform them on the caveat that he trains you first to ensure you're up to it vocally."

I'm silent as I try to digest everything this man has thrown at me. Based on one video, this high-profile composer, whose name I should recognize, has decided he wants to train me and have me perform his top-secret compositions he won't let anyone else perform?

Jenkins clears his throat when I'm silent for so long. "Miss Young, this is the equivalent of a Juilliard scholarship—if not better—because you'd be receiving one-on-one training from a musical genius. It's the opportunity of a lifetime."

"I don't know what to say," I tell him honestly when I finally gather my wits enough to formulate words.

I advise you to say yes," he prompts.

I stammer, unsure what to say. This is a huge decision, and I don't know where to begin. My head is spinning. "Can I have some time to think about it?"

Jenkins smiles at me indulgently. "How about I come back tomorrow for your answer?" he suggests.

He stands and leaves before I get a chance to say anything else.

I'm still sitting in the booth, completely stupefied, when Meg runs over and quirks an inquisitive eyebrow at me. "What was that all about?"

"He says some high-profile composer wants to train me," I tell my friend dubiously. "His name is Erik Duvall."

Meg's mouth falls open, and she plops down into the booth across from me. "Erik Duvall?" she stage whispers.

Okay, I feel stupid now because it's obvious Erik Duvall is a name I should know. I shake my head dazedly. "Who is he?"

Meg reaches across the table and takes my hands in hers, squeezing them gently as she leans forward and tells me earnestly, "Harper, you have to take this opportunity. He's the best composer alive. I swear the man is up there with Beethoven or Mozart." She does a little dance in her seat and squeals, "See! I told you you're an amazing singer!"

"But what if I disappoint him?" I voice my worries. "I mean, what if I'm not that good in person, Meg? What if it was just the video or—"

Meg interrupts me with a scoff. "Stop trying to downplay your talent, Harper." She scowls at me. "You're amazing, and everybody knows it but you. This just proves it. I hope you told that guy yes."

I shake my head at her. "I asked for time to think about it."

Meg's face pales. "Oh, my god," she mumbles as if I've blown my opportunity. "Should I run after him?" She moves to get up, but I place a hand on her wrist.

"No." I shake my head. "He said he'd be here tomorrow."

Meg calms down at that. "Okay, so tomorrow when he comes in here, you tell him hell, yes, you'll do it."

"But I don't know what this entails," I point out.

"Who cares?" Meg is practically screaming at me. "It's Erik fucking Duvall! You know he never lets anyone perform his compositions, right?"

"So I've heard," I say thoughtfully.

Meg goes on like I never said a word. "He's so reclusive no one knows what he looks like. Hell, you should do it just to solve the mystery of who he is."

I see the manager frowning at us from behind the counter. She makes an up motion with her finger. "Back to work, ladies! Breaktime is over."

Meg glances at me as we both hurry to stand and get back to work. "Seriously, Harper. Do this. Do this for yourself. Do it for your father. He'd be so proud of you for getting the attention of a man like Duvall."

I chew on my lip as I go about the rest of my day, considering her words.

I do a search for Erik Duvall on the internet during my next break. I can't find any pictures of him, but there are plenty of write-ups about his music in various magazines. It looks like it's all true. He's the best of the best when it comes to music.

I'd be a fool to turn an opportunity like this down, but part of me is scared of failure.

Another part of me knows that I'll always regret it if I don't at least try to seize this opportunity. I chew on my lip as I continue to contemplate all my options.

I finally square my shoulders and inhale a deep breath.

I'm going to tell Jenkins yes tomorrow.

A flutter of excitement lights in my breast.

I'm really doing this.

***

Erik

I pace the floor impatiently, more nervous than I can ever remember being in my entire life. At the same time, I'm flooded with a sense of anticipation. I'm worse than a high school boy on his first date.

I think this fluttering in my stomach is called butterflies, though I can't remember having them before. It's honestly a bit nauseating, and I feel like it will only settle when I finally have her in front of me.

Harper. My little angel. I almost dropped to the floor in gratitude when Jenkins called me and affirmed that she said yes.

She said yes.

I haven't experienced the joy I felt at that confirmation since before the war. Hell, I haven't felt this alive since I came back from overseas.

I finally hear a knock at my door and stop pacing, running a hand over my cropped hair.

"Enter!" My voice comes out as a bark.

My heart is thudding in my chest as Jenkins opens the door and gives me a slight nod before he steps back to reveal Harper. I vaguely register my head of security closing the door behind him as he leaves us alone in the room.

My eyes are pinned on her. My god, she's even more breathtaking in person. Her chocolate curls glint with golden highlights in the sunlight streaming through the open curtains. I'm generally not one to let in any sunlight, but my study was so dark it looked like a tomb, and I didn't want Harper to be wary of the dimly lit space.

She's like a flower. She needs sunlight. I instinctively know this.

She's dressed in a simple pair of leggings and an off-the-shoulder top. She's so young and fresh and vibrant that I ache looking at her. Her entire *existence* hurts me. My fingers twitch with the need to touch her skin and see if she's just as petal soft as she looks. I want to run my fingers through her hair and feel it glide through them like silk.

I take a deep breath, inhaling her scent. She smells like fresh berries. She's everything young and sweet and innocent.

"Harper," I say her name reverently. I don't even bother with the formality of calling her Miss Young. We're going to be on a first-name basis because I feel like I'll die if I don't hear my name on her lips soon.

She clasps her hands together in front of herself nervously and shifts from foot to foot.

"I'm Erik Duvall," I introduce myself, stepping out of the shadows to get this part over with.

She lets out a tiny gasp, and her eyes widen as she takes in my scarred visage.

My heart plummets, though her reaction is no more than I expected. My lips press into a thin line as my heart bottoms out. Her reaction only reaffirms what I already knew. I'm too hideous for her.

To her credit, she gathers herself quickly and smiles at me. My god, it's the most beautiful smile I've ever seen. It warms me from the inside out.

"Hello, Mr. Duvall. Thank you so much for this opportunity." Her voice is pure music, even when she's just speaking.

"Please call me Erik." My voice comes out choked, and she gives me a curious look before I clear my throat and repeat myself.

"Please, call me Erik." There. I didn't sound like a dying animal that time.

"Okay, Erik."

I grip the side of my desk to keep from falling over. Hearing my name in that musical voice is almost enough to make me come on the spot. I can only imagine what it would sound like to hear her moaning it while I take her to the heights of ecstasy.

She shifts on her feet again, drawing me back to the present. *Fuck.* It's going to take every ounce of control I have to keep my hands off her and stay focused enough to train her.

A flutter of excitement runs through me at the thought of training her. I long to be in her presence. She has a rare gift, and the composer in me is overjoyed at the thought of molding that voice for me and me alone. I'm eager to help her hone it and reach her highest potential.

That's what she's here for, I remind myself sternly. She's here for training—not to fulfill my wildest fantasies.

"I'm so pleased you accepted my offer. Your voice is a rare gift," I tell her genuinely. "I look forward to helping you hone it."

Her cheeks flush under the praise, and she looks up at me shyly. "Really?"

My god, does she not know how good she is? Seeing the innocent and almost embarrassed way she looks at me lets me know that she doesn't.

"Harper," I tell her seriously, "you have the most magnificent voice I've ever heard, and I don't say that lightly."

I truly don't. I'm not a man who gives out many compliments. She smiles at me again, and I know at this moment that I'd rip out my heart and hand it to her if she asked for it. There's nothing I won't do for this tiny angel.

I clear my throat. "Shall we begin?"

She smiles that radiant smile at me and nods her head eagerly.

I stare at her in awe as I lead her through the scales so I can determine her range.

I haven't been living up until this moment. This girl is my reason for living. Everything in my life has been leading up to this, and I vow that I will do everything within my power to make her the star she deserves to be.

CHAPTER 4

Harper

ERIK DUVALL IS nothing like I imagined. I don't know what I expected, but the scarred yet dangerously handsome man in front of me isn't it.

I see why there aren't any pictures of him online. He probably makes it a point to stay away from the cameras, and who could blame him? The whole right side of his face is crisscrossed with scars, and I can't help but wonder how he got them, though I would never ask him.

His biography online mentioned that he was in the Marines several years ago, and I can only assume that his scars are battle scars. While some people might find the scars unpleasant, to me, they're mesmerizing. He's like a fearsome warrior.

He's tall and extremely well-built. He probably keeps whatever workout routine he was used to in the military.

His hair is cropped close to his head, and his arms and chest are so buff that I can practically see the fabric of his long-sleeved button-up straining with the effort of containing all that muscle. There's not an ounce of fat on the man.

He's huge, and while I'm not the shortest girl in the world, the way he towers over me makes me feel tiny.

Everything about him is dark and dangerous and powerful—everything except his eyes which are a clear blue. They stand out in stark contrast to his dark hair, washing over me like ocean waves.

Erik looks at me more intensely than anyone I've ever met. His gaze pierces me like he's trying to see deep into my heart. He's not just looking at the surface. He's looking at my soul.

And I don't know what it is about him, but he exudes this raw masculinity. If anything, his scars only make him more alluring. He's beautiful, and I'm completely in awe of him, especially whenever he opens his mouth and sings. My jaw nearly dropped to the floor when I heard his voice for the first time.

He has the smoothest, richest male voice I've ever heard. He's a thousand times better than all the male voices trending in the charts right now. Why the hell he's not a professional singer is beyond me because he certainly has the talent and the voice for it.

When he told me I was the perfect soprano, I practically glowed under his praise, and the look on his face when he pushed me to see how high my range was and discovered I could hit a high E was a balm to my shy heart.

Erik is nothing short of a perfect tenor. When he sings, I'm in complete awe of him. He sings with such passion it makes my heart gallop away in my chest and my blood hum.

His voice is dark and rich and sensual. It envelops me like a physical caress. It's an erotic experience, and that makes me blush because he's my teacher. He wants to train me so I can perform his work for him. Nothing more.

He's a very strict teacher. Oh, he's not unkind, but he's focused, and he makes me want to do my best to please him.

He trains me all day. I put in a temporary leave of absence at my workplace when Erik told me that if I wanted to do this, he needed one hundred percent focus and dedication. He insisted on paying for my training, and the sum he deposited into my bank account on the first day had my jaw hitting the floor.

I arrive at his place early each morning, and I don't leave until late in the evening. We work on and off all day with him giving me breaks to rest my voice and drink plenty of water, teas, and other approved beverages.

He sends Jenkins to pick me up and take me home, insisting that he drive me so I don't have to rely on public transportation. I'm grateful because it saves me the expense and hassle.

I pinch myself now and then to make sure this is real because I can't believe this man found me and decided to give me this fantastic opportunity based on one video.

I've learned so much in such a short time. That's how competent a teacher he is.

"Almost," his smooth voice tells me as I sing the last line of the song we've been practicing. "You have to control your breathing. Your posture makes all the difference. Here."

Erik walks up behind me, and I'm engulfed by his expensive bergamot and sandalwood cologne. He circles me with an arm and places a hand across my stomach. I can't help but notice how his huge hand almost dwarfs my entire abdomen. My breath hitches at the contact as he pulls me closer to him. There's scarcely an inch of space between my back and his chest, and heat emanates from him like a furnace.

"Here." His voice is low and husky as he speaks close to my ear, his fingers tightening slightly on my stomach. "Sing from here. Feel it rise within you."

When he makes no move to release me, I realize he wants me to do it while his hand is on me like this.

My voice is shaky from the sensations fluttering through me at his proximity. It wobbles as it emerges from my throat, but then he begins to hum the melody in my ear. I follow along with him perfectly, my voice melding with his. Relaxing in his hold, I give myself over to his voice, my own following it like a bird taking flight. I feel the music burst up from my stomach and shoot through the top of my head. It's as if his hand is coaxing the melody from deep within me. The sensation is unlike anything I've ever felt before.

The note dies off perfectly. My voice soared higher than I ever imagined it could, and I know I've done well. It was amazing to have the notes move through me so effortlessly.

"Erik!" I gasp out his name. I hold my hand to my throat, twisting in his arms to look up at him in wonder.

He's looking down at me, his eyes filled with pride

and something else I can't identify, something that warms my belly and makes my breath hitch in my throat.

"Brava, my little songbird," he praises me with a tip of his lips.

I blush and grin widely. I love Erik's nickname for me. I don't know exactly when it started, but he calls me his little songbird all the time now. Oh, I'm sure he doesn't mean it the way it sounds, but I like the thought of being *his* songbird.

Erik's arms are still wrapped around my waist. He seems to realize this the same time I do because he clears his throat and steps back.

I don't know why I feel a twinge of disappointment at seeing him retreat. He walks over and seats himself at the piano before glancing at me, back in teacher mode. "From the beginning of the aria, then."

I nod and bite my lip, waiting for my cue. When I sing this time, I remember what he showed me, and the notes flow from me effortlessly as I recall the sensation of his hand on my stomach.

Everyone said Erik was a musical genius, and they weren't kidding. He spent some of that first day letting me hear him play the piano while he sang some of his lyrics, and my gosh, the man's music is astounding. I am humbled and honored that he chose me to sing it for him.

It's not opera or classical music, but it's also not the mainstream music you hear on the radio. It's classy and fluid and beautiful. Erik writes symphonies and arias, but he puts a unique twist on them. They're like nothing I've ever heard, and the melodies linger in my head.

I'm loving every minute of this. I love Erik's music. I love the training. I love just spending time with him.

Erik knows precisely how to challenge me and help me improve.

Finally, I'm no longer lonely.

I never want this to end.

CHAPTER 5

Erik

TRAINING HARPER IS A BREEZE. She's an eager student, and she learns quickly. I love seeing the flush of pleasure on her face when her voice soars higher than she thought possible. That little moment of surprised elation in her eyes makes the torture of not claiming her like a beast in heat worthwhile.

Everything about her is tempting. Although she's thin, she has curves in all the right places. I can't keep my eyes off her perfect body. Her hair taunts me, and I want to bury my fingers in it.

And her eyes...dear god, those eyes...they're my favorite thing of all, those windows to her soul. They're big and brown and framed by dark, thick lashes. Against her creamy skin and puffy pink lips, they make her look like one of those fragile porcelain dolls my mother collected, especially with her long curly hair that flows down to her waist. Coupled with her angelic voice and perfect coloratura, she's my fantasy come to life.

She's almost ready for her debut, and while I'm proud of her and want to show off her voice, another part of me selfishly wants to keep her all to myself.

Harper never asks me for a break, trusting me to know when her voice is tiring. I'm so in tune with every nuance of her voice that I can always tell when she's straining and needs to rest for a little while.

"Okay, that's enough for now," I tell her after the last note of the song we've been working on fades away.

Her shoulders instantly relax, and she gives me a grateful smile. My heart clenches every time the woman smiles at me.

"How about we go into the kitchen and get something to eat?"

She nods her head eagerly. We walk side by side to my kitchen as we've done for several days now. I pull out a fruit tray, knowing that's what she likes best, and it's good for her voice since fruit is full of water.

She bites into a piece of pineapple, and the juices

drip onto her chin. She moans appreciatively and closes her eyes as if in ecstasy.

My throat goes dry as I watch her. I never thought consuming food was a particularly erotic activity until I watched Harper do it. Of course, everything she does turns me on. Even a simple flip of her hair away from her neck is enticing.

I plop my piece of pineapple into my mouth to try to distract myself from my suddenly raging hard-on. I regard her thoughtfully as she eats a few grapes and then a strawberry.

She smiles when she sees me watching her. She's so at ease with me now, and while I'm thankful for that, it astounds me too. I haven't been around people for so long that I don't know if she understands the gift she's bestowing on me by spending time with me each day.

She brightens my day. These past few weeks of training her have been nothing short of the highlight of my life.

My heart falls at the thought of it being over soon.

But it doesn't have to be. I quickly remind myself.

Vocalists always need to train and improve their craft. I can keep this going indefinitely—even after she makes her debut. She'll still need to practice. I can be her teacher from here on out. A rush of joy goes

through me at the thought of keeping her forever—
even if it is only in this capacity.

"I have your debut scheduled for Friday." I finally
tell her the news I've been debating sharing with her
all day.

Her hand stops midway to her open mouth, and
her eyes widen as she looks at me. I expected her to be
excited, but she chews on her lip nervously and casts
an uncertain glance at me.

"Are you sure I'm ready?" she asks skeptically.

"You were born ready," I tell her seriously. "A voice
like yours can't be manufactured, Harper. All I've been
doing is teaching you how to use it better."

She nods, her face flushing. Still, she looks down,
looking troubled.

I frown. I thought she'd be happy about this news.
"What is it, Harper? Is something wrong?"

She looks up at me from beneath lowered lashes
before she finally admits softly, "What if I disappoint
you?"

It's like someone has knocked the wind out of me.
My precious little songbird. "You could never disappoint me," I tell her honestly.

When she still doesn't look up at me, I can't resist.
Everything inside me is telling me to comfort her, so I

reach out to grasp her chin and gently tilt it up so she's looking at me.

Again, I marvel at how she doesn't recoil from my touch. Do I just imagine it, or does she lean into it? Surely, I just imagined that.

She looks up at me, her eyes wide and luminous and so deep I could drown in them.

"I know you've heard the rumors that I've never let anyone perform my work before."

She looks at me solemnly.

"Well, it's all true," I tell her. "I've never entrusted my work with anyone."

A flash of panic flares in her eyes, but I rush to reassure her, "I'm not telling you this to put pressure on you. I'm telling you because I would only entrust it to someone I knew could do it justice, and Harper, I have complete faith in you. You just need to believe in yourself. If I didn't think you were ready, I wouldn't put you out there."

I fight back a groan as she bites her bottom lip. I release her chin, afraid that if I keep touching her, I'll give in to my baser urge to press my lips against hers and find out if she tastes just as sweet as she looks.

"Do you trust me?"

She doesn't even hesitate before she nods. "Yes," she whispers.

My breath catches in my throat. I'm humbled by how quickly she supplied her answer.

How did I get this lucky? Even if this is all we ever are—and this *is* all we ever will be because I am nowhere near good enough for her—Harper has made my life worth living. She is everything, and she will have everything her little heart desires if I have anything to say about it.

"Erik?" She says my name softly, and my ears practically melt. I'll never tire of hearing my name dripping from her pretty little lips.

"Yes." I raise my eyebrows at her.

She bites that bottom lip again, and it takes everything in me to keep from biting it myself. "I'm scared," she confesses.

I don't say anything for a moment. I'm trying to think of how to soothe her fears without invalidating them.

She takes my silence for something else because she adds, "I know it's silly of me, but have you ever been scared?"

She looks up at me with those big brown eyes, and I find myself admitting something to her I've never told anyone else before. "Yes, I have. During the war."

Her eyes go wide, and then she says softly, "I'm so sorry. You must think I'm ridiculous for being scared of something like singing professionally in front of people for the first time when you went through something so horrible."

I reach across the table and take her hands, following instincts that tell me to touch her and communicate with her that I understand her fear even though it's not the same as mine.

"You're not silly, and there's nothing wrong with fear. It's healthy." I look past her, seeing the battlefield before me in my mind's eye. "It's those who have no fear we should worry about."

I consider my next words carefully, deciding how much to share with her. I've never wanted to talk about my experience with anyone before, but I want Harper to know that she can trust me. I want her to know she can tell me anything. Having her share her fears with me like this is a gift. It shows how much she trusts me.

I feel it's only fair to do the same with her. "The war was horrible," I tell her honestly. "I was terrified for days on end, and when the explosion happened," I indicate my face, "well, I'm sure you can figure out the rest."

The shrapnel cut me up like a thousand tiny knives. I still remember the pain of it cutting into my skin, but it must have damaged some of the nerves because I don't have much pain.

Harper has never asked me about my face, and I've been grateful for that. She never makes me feel like a freak or less of a man. After her initial reaction, she's never looked at me strangely. Not once.

She studies my face, but I don't see fear or revulsion in her eyes. It's not pity either. I'm glad because I don't want her pity. No, it's a quiet sadness.

"Does it hurt?" she asks softly.

I pause. No one has ever asked me that before. I've had plenty of people ask me what happened, but not Harper. She didn't press me to tell her what had happened. I told her of my own accord. No, when my precious little songbird asks me a question about my face, she's asking me how I feel. She's asking out of concern for me, not to sate her curiosity.

If I didn't know I was hopelessly in love with her, I would now.

"No, little songbird," I tell her as I gently stroke the pad of my thumb over her palm. "It doesn't hurt."

She gives me a tiny, beautiful smile. "I'm glad."

We sit there in companionable silence for a few moments. Neither of us speaks, but we don't need to. Something passes between us, something that binds us closer together, and I know by the way her pretty little eyes look directly into mine that she feels it too.

"Let's get back to practice," I finally tell her.

She immediately moves to obey me with complete trust, ready to follow my lead.

I'm not ready to relinquish this moment between us, but it's either that or me giving in to my desire to lean across this table and kiss her for all she's worth.

CHAPTER 6

Harper

SOMETHING SHIFTED between Erik and me in the kitchen. He shared something with me that I suspect he's never shared with anyone else, and it humbles me more than I can say. It also makes my heart float to know that he believes in me.

I'm determined that I won't let him down on Friday. When I sing, I'm going to be singing only for him. I'll pour my heart and soul into every note to make him proud and do his music justice.

When we go back to his music room, Erik takes his place at the piano, and I stand beside him as I always do. He begins to play, and I watch as his long fingers dance over the keys. Something about the way his fingers move so deftly causes my stomach to clench. His hands are so masculine and yet so fluid. My cheeks flush as I remember what they felt like splayed across my stomach.

I'm so distracted by my heated thoughts that I miss my opening cue. Erik looks up at me and raises an eyebrow. He begins to sing, nodding at me encouragingly and leading me with his voice.

I follow along effortlessly, but he doesn't stop singing. He keeps singing along with me. Our voices meld together and become one, and it's like nothing I've ever experienced before.

I'm drawn to him, stepping closer and closer until I slide down onto the piano bench next to him.

He doesn't stop playing, yet he's not looking at the keys. He turns and holds my eyes with his own as he continues to play, his voice becoming even more sensual as he sings while looking right into my eyes. I don't know what this is passing between us, but it's like our souls are entwined in song. It's so captivating that I almost feel dizzy.

When our last notes fade away, we stare at one another, our chests heaving. Erik's nostrils flare as his eyes flick down to my lips. I tilt my head ever so slightly, my lips tingling, wanting to feel his mouth on mine.

As if he can sense my desire, he chokes out my name. "Harper."

"Erik," I speak his name breathlessly, and then his lips are on mine.

And holy cow, it's amazing. I've never been kissed like this before.

Erik kisses me deeply, slipping his tongue into my mouth to twine with mine. It's hot and erotic, and it causes an ache to bloom between my thighs.

I let out a little whimper, and he wraps his arms around me, pulling me flush against him on the bench. I press into him so my breasts are crushed against his hard chest. I need to get closer, closer to him, so I can melt into him completely.

He groans into my mouth, and I feel that rumble deep down in my soul. It does something to me, makes me wild. I cup his face, stroking my hands over his cheeks—the smooth and the scarred—marveling at the difference in texture.

When Erik feels my hand against his scarred cheek, he raises his to cover mine, pulling back just enough to whisper wonderingly against my lips, "How can you touch me like this, Harper? Don't you see how hideously scarred I am? And look at you. Jesus, you're so beautiful. So perfect. Not a mar on your body."

My heart swells within me at the naked vulnerability in his tone. Here he is, this big, powerful man, yet he's showing me a side of him that I know he's never shown anyone else. He's allowing himself to be vulnerable around me, and I won't waste this precious gift he's given me.

Instead, I gently press my lips against his again before I pull back and look directly into his eyes. "You are beautiful, Erik. Everything about you. Yes, you've got scars, but they prove how wonderful you are inside. They don't diminish your beauty. They enhance it."

I see moisture shimmering in his eyes before he mumbles, "Fuck, Harper."

And then his lips are on me again—only this time they're not only on my lips but also trailing along my jaw and the column of my neck. I tilt my head to the side to give him greater access to me, loving the sensation of his lips on my flesh. He licks and sucks and nips at my throat, sending tingles shooting through me. I've never been drunk before, but I've been tipsy. The sensations Erik is eliciting are reminiscent of that deliciously lightheaded feeling from the high of alcohol—only this high is a million times better.

I let out a squeak of surprise as Erik suddenly pulls me onto his lap so that I'm straddling him.

"Fuck, I can't get close enough to you, sweetheart," he whispers against my ear, mirroring my thoughts from earlier.

I gasp as I feel the hard bulge protruding from his pants. I feel an answering throb deep within me, and I move against it instinctively.

Erik hisses in a breath and clamps a hand on my hip to still me. "Oh, sweet Jesus, you can't do that, baby."

I look down at him and flush, wondering if I was doing something wrong.

He lets out a little chuckle at the look on my face. He must be able to read my thoughts because he says, "It's too much. You're too perfect. If you keep doing that, I'm afraid I'll embarrass myself."

My flush only deepens when I realize what he means. "I'm sorry," I stammer as I try to climb off him.

He clasps his hands around my waist, keeping me in place. "Where do you think you're going?"

I look at him and bite my lip. "I don't want to cause you pain."

He lets out an incredulous chuckle. "The only way you cause me pain, sweetheart, is to deny me."

Before I can ask him what he means, he crashes his

lips back on mine, and then his hands are on me, trailing all over my skin, cupping my breasts. He flicks his thumbs back and forth over my nipples, and I moan at how painfully, deliciously hard the little buds get.

"Shit, sweetheart," he groans as he yanks down my shirt and takes the hardened bud in his mouth.

My head falls back and I turn myself over to the sensation. I never knew it could feel so good to have a man's mouth on me like this. A hot wire connects everywhere his lips touch to the bundle of nerves between my legs.

As if he can sense that, Erik's hand moves under the seam of my leggings and down to that throbbing area between my legs. "Christ, Harper, how are you this wet for *me?*"

He says "for me" incredulously like he can't believe he could be the one to elicit such a reaction from someone. My heart wrenches as I realize that this man is so insecure because of his scars that he has no idea how insanely hot he is.

I take his face in my hands again and look him in the eyes. "Even with the scars, you can have any woman you want. You're insanely hot, Erik." I shake my head. "I can't believe *you* want *me.*"

I don't know if he believes me, but his eyes darken. "All I want is you, Harper. Only you. It's only ever been you. From the first moment I heard you sing, I knew I wanted you to be mine."

My heart does a little flip at his admission.

"Call it crazy, but I felt this connection with you the first moment I saw you on the TV singing your little heart out," he goes on.

"Erik," I whisper his name tremulously before he begins to move his finger over my slick folds. I let out a moan whenever he hits a spot that sends tingles shooting through me.

Encouraged, he rubs that spot in little circles until he has me panting and straining against him.

"That's it. Come for me, little songbird," he bites out as if he's in pain.

Apparently, all I needed was his encouragement because I'm suddenly shattering into a thousand pieces. I ride his hand wildly, following some deep instinct as muscles I never even knew I had convulse around air.

"Erik!" I scream his name as my release washes over me.

"Fuck!" he growls.

He suddenly rips his pants open and pulls my leggings down before seating me on top of him. I've never seen a man's naked flesh up close before, but I don't even get a chance to look at Erik before I feel him prodding against my opening.

My eyes widen at the sudden fullness as his head pops in. He feels large—*really* large—so much so that I'm starting to doubt whether this will work.

"Erik," I breathe out his name shakily, getting ready to tell him that maybe he won't fit.

But his eyes are wild, and he doesn't hear the hesitation in my voice because his jaw clenches before he suddenly thrusts up into me while pulling me down on him.

I scream out as a sharp pain pierces me. He lets out a strangled groan and stares at me in amazement and horror.

He pulls back the slightest bit to look in between our bodies. When he sees the blood coating his cock, he turns his concerned eyes on me. "Christ, Harper, you're a virgin. Why didn't you tell me, sweetheart?"

His eyes are full of regret, and I flush. Is he disappointed that I don't have any experience? Did he not want a virgin?

"I tried to," I pant, struggling to adjust to his girth.

"Fuck me," he curses himself. "I should be drug out into the street and shot for taking you so roughly. I swear I had no idea, sweetheart. If I had, I never would have—"

I cut him off by pressing a finger against his lips. "The pain has faded, but I'm sorry if I'm not what you want. I'm not a practiced lover or anything—"

Erik lets out an incredulous chuckle. "Are you kidding me? I'm happy as hell no one else has been inside this tight little pussy." I feel him jerk inside me. "It's all mine," he breathes into my ear.

A shiver runs down my spine and there's an intense pressure deep inside me. I'm full of him, connected to him, and it feels incredible. I wiggle around, moving instinctively. Oh, good lord. I bite my lip and moan at the friction of him sliding inside me.

He moans, too, his head falling back, the muscles in his neck taut.

"Damn, Harper, you feel so good," he grits out.

"Erik, please," I beg him. I'm not sure exactly what I'm begging for, but I know that whatever it is, he can give it to me.

Erik's jaw firms as he looks down at me. "Don't worry, little girl. I'm going to give you exactly what you need."

He begins to push up into me while rocking me gently on him. Every nerve ending in my body is snapping with pleasure as he rocks slowly in and out of me. He's holding my eyes with his beautiful blue ones, staring intently into them as he moves within me, making this nothing short of the most intimate experience of my life.

I clench around him involuntarily at the heated look in his eyes. His breath catches, and his eyes take on a feral look as he begins to pick up the pace.

My hand falls back onto the piano keys. Discordant notes pierce the room. The sound only seems to spur Erik on.

He stands and lays me over the keys as he continues to drive up into me, our bodies hitting disjointed note after disjoined note while creating a beautiful symphony all our own.

The music is hot and pulses like our bodies. Erik seems to swell even more, and the pressure inside me grows. I clutch his shoulders, my legs wrapped around him as he hammers into me.

"Fuck, Harper, you've been saving this little virgin pussy for me, haven't you?" he rasps right in my ear. "Saving it all for me because you knew I would take care of it. And I'll take care of you too. Fuck, I'll do anything for you, baby. Anything. Just say you're mine. Say you'll never leave me." His voice is desperate, and I cling to him, my arms wrapped around his neck as I hold him tight.

"Tell me you're mine, little girl. Fuck, I need to hear it." His voice is pleading, and I can't deny him, especially when it's what I feel down deep in my soul.

"Yes, I'm yours," I agree breathlessly.

"Mine," he chokes out in my ear as he rams up into me even harder.

The piano keys are digging into my backside, but I don't care. The pressure within me is building and swelling. "Erik!" I call out his name, begging him.

"Yes, I know, baby. I know what you need, and I'm going to give it to you. You don't have to worry about anything anymore. If this sweet little pussy needs anything, you bring it to me, and I'll take care of you. I'll sit you right on this piano bench, and you can bounce all over your man's dick as much as you want."

I don't know if it's the way he's stabbing into me or the filthy words he's breathing right into my ear. Maybe it's a combination of both, but it pushes me over the edge.

Suddenly, I'm soaring into outer space as my entire body spasms in a blinding pleasure unlike anything I've ever known. This orgasm is much more intense than the one he gave me earlier with his fingers.

"Yes, yes, that's it, sweetheart," he chants in my ear. "So perfect, my angel, my sweetheart, my little song-bird, my little girl."

He's blabbering nonsense in my ear, his breath

coming out in hoarse pants until he finally roars my name.

He swells inside me, and I feel his heated release flooding me. The sensation of his cum jetting into me sends me spiraling into another orgasm until we're quaking against one another.

I lay lax in Erik's arms with him seated inside me as we both come down from our climaxes.

He strokes his hands through my hair and drops kisses over my forehead, cheeks, and lips while whispering words of endearment to me. "Good girl. So perfect. Took me so good, my little angel. Never going to let you go. Going to take care of you forever."

I tighten my arms around his neck and bury my face in his chest, letting his praise wash over me, his words more musical and beautiful than the finest symphony.

Erik

HARPER HAS STAYED with me every night since I claimed her innocence for my own. I wouldn't hear of her leaving me.

Holding her in my arms all night is like a dream come true. It's more than I ever dared to hope for.

While she sleeps, I lay there and watch every rise and fall of her chest, every little puff of breath she takes. She's so precious. I don't want to fall asleep or miss a moment of watching her. I could watch her all day, every day, and be content with that.

But I love hearing her sing. Her voice is like nothing else on this earth, and knowing that she's singing my music—and *only* my music—sends a primitive sense of satisfaction through me.

We spend every moment together, getting closer than I ever thought it was possible to be to another person.

I take her in every room of the house, although I make sure to keep up on her training. I can't keep my hands off her, though, so during our breaks, I bend her over the piano or take her up against the wall or over the kitchen counter.

I've put her in every position known to man—and then some. But I can't help it. I can't resist her. I've been sexually starved for years, but I've been starved for Harper for a lifetime.

The day is finally upon us, though, when I have to share her with the world. I both anticipate and dread her debut.

Harper wants me to go with her. I know she does, but sweet girl that she is, she won't press me to push my boundaries. She merely asked me if I would be there, and when I told her that I would be watching, I know she got my meaning.

My heart squeezes at the thought of not physically being there for her, but I haven't been in a crowd in years. I like to stay hidden away in my mansion. I hate the thought of showing my scarred face. I grimace, thinking about all the questions I'd have to endure.

I can't go on camera with her, but I hate to send her by herself. She doesn't seem to hold it against me, thank god. She gives me a gentle kiss on the lips before Jenkins drives her to the studio where she's going to be making her live debut.

I'm glued to the TV from the moment she leaves the house. When she walks out in the white floor-length gown we selected for her to wear, my mouth goes dry. I'm having second thoughts about letting her wear something like that without me there to protect her.

Fuck, she looks like an angel sent down from heaven. She's so young and beautiful and vibrant, with her chocolate curls falling to her tiny waist. There's no way in hell every man in the studio isn't going to want her. Jealousy surges through me, hot and potent, but I try my best to tamp it down, reminding myself that it's my bed she's been in for days now.

When she opens her mouth and sings my composition—something I've never allowed to be performed publicly by anyone—my soul soars within me. She's radiant, especially at that moment when her eyes look directly into the camera. My heart jumps into my throat. It might seem crazy, but I know that look was for me. She's singing for *me*. I can't wipe the idiotic grin off my face.

Even though I'm alone in my home, I applaud her loudly when it's over. Fuck, I wish I was there so I could pull her into my arms the moment she comes off stage.

I frown when she starts to leave the stage and is suddenly held back by the host of the evening. He stays her with a hand on her arm, and anger flares in my chest that he has the audacity to touch her. She turns with an inquisitive look, and I lean forward in my chair as I stare daggers at the screen.

"We've got a super special surprise for you tonight," the host announces. "We've brought on a special guest to sing an impromptu duet with Miss Young."

Harper looks just as shocked as I am. Of course, I'm pissed as hell. I was not briefed about any of this. Harper was supposed to sing solo, and that's it. She's not supposed to sing a duet with anyone.

"What do you say, Harper?" The host gives her a wide smile, and before she can answer, her duet partner is announced.

My anger skyrockets when I see the young punk who walks out onto the stage. Brad Baker. I know he's some up-and-coming hotshot tenor in his early twenties. He's heartbreakingly handsome, the latest heart-throb and playboy in the music scene.

I fist my hands together when I see him look over at *my* Harper, the look of appreciation evident in his eyes.

Fuck no. I do *not* want her singing with him. I begin to pace the floor restlessly, cursing at the top of my lungs.

Fuck!

There's nothing I can do. I consider getting the producer on the phone, but the performance is already underway.

My heart clenches as I watch my angel singing with another man. I know it's not her fault. I know there was no way she could politely decline. I never briefed her on how to handle a situation like this because I never foresaw it happening. No, she couldn't refuse without making a scene and ruining the success of her debut.

Still, I hate it when I hear her voice melding with his. Her voice is only ever supposed to be joined with mine. *Mine!*

My vision goes red whenever Brad reaches out and takes her hand, looking directly into her eyes as they sing the popular love song as if they are truly in love.

When they reach the end of the song, he lifts her hand to his lips and places a kiss on her knuckles.

I lose it and overturn the coffee table. Shit goes flying everywhere, but I don't give a fuck. I have to burn off this rage somehow.

I pour myself a drink to try to calm my nerves, but I only get angrier as I knock it back, so I pour myself another—and another.

I haven't gotten drunk since before I went into the military, and I know I'm well on my way, but fuck, what does it matter now? I'm still watching the media coverage after Harper and Brad's performance, and of course, the reporters are already trying to find the hidden romance between the two of them.

They play that motherfucking clip of them singing together over and over again. They keep talking about the emotion between them and how real it seemed, and what if there is something there? What if they've been secretly dating all this time?

I start to have my own doubts. What if she *is* secretly in love with him? What if they've known each other for a while, and I'm just the idiot who didn't know it? They certainly look like the perfect couple.

I raise a hand to my scarred face and frown. I remember the kind words she said to me right before she let me make love to her. What if that was all just a student trying to get ahead? Worse, what if she only let me touch her because she felt sorry for me or because I took advantage of her? Doesn't that make more sense than her wanting me?

Why would she want someone like me? I'm nowhere near as attractive as young Brad. My lip curls in disgust as I eye his image on the screen.

I throw the glass, the contents and all, across the room, and it shatters to the floor. That has to be the fifth one I've broken tonight.

I pour myself another drink. She's still not home. Why is she not back? She said she'd come back to me. Maybe she changed her mind. Maybe she's out with *Brad.*

I snarl at the thought, but my face falls as my heart becomes heavy.

My little songbird...

God only knows how much I want to keep her. Guilt consumes me. Now that the world has had a taste of her, they're not going to let her go.

And it's all my fault. Part of me knows that. The respectable thing for me to do is to set her free. Let her live her life without a monster like me chaining her down.

But then there's the part of me that's balking at the thought of ever letting her go, screaming at me to hold her to her promise when she told me she was mine.

That's why when she walks in the door, my anger has long since passed, and I'm left with nothing but a hollow resignation.

She's glowing, and who am I to dim her light?

"Oh, Erik, it was wonderful!" she babbles, her eyes shining as she tells me all about her night.

I listened to her half-heartedly. I'm happy for her, but my heart is breaking.

She finally frowns when she realizes I'm not saying anything. "Erik, what's wrong?"

She sits down next to me, and I scoot away from her, knowing that if I allow her to get too near—if her sweet berry scent surrounds me—I might not have the strength to do what I know I must.

Her eyes take on a hurt look when I move away from her. She looks so concerned that I can almost believe it's real. And hell, even if it is, this can't work. I've been living in a fantasy to think it could.

"You did well tonight, my little songbird," I tell her, my heart aching at my nickname for her, "but our training is over now. There's nothing else I can teach you."

Her eyes widen as she looks at me. "You mean you want me to go?"

I don't speak at first. I can't lie to her because I don't want her to go. Instead, I say, "It's for the best."

"Have I done something wrong?" she asks, her voice shaky.

I take a deep breath before I answer simply. "No."

I see her eyes begin to shimmer with tears when I don't offer any further explanation, and I look away. She's better off without me. She'll be better off with someone like Brad.

"Thank you for everything you've done for me," she says softly before she gets up and walks out of the room, taking my heart with her.

When I hear my front door close, the rage comes crashing back down on me, and I destroy the rest of my study while I roar out my pain and heartbreak.

CHAPTER 8

Harper

MY HEART IS BROKEN. I can't believe Erik sent me away. I thought we had something special, but maybe I'm just a naive little girl. Maybe he was disappointed in my inexperience. Maybe I imagined everything that happened between us, the vulnerability, the way he seemed to genuinely care about me.

Maybe he just wanted to get his rocks off, and I was a convenient choice.

I want to be angry with him, but I'd be lying if I said I didn't miss him. I miss him so much it hurts.

So I keep myself busy. Since my debut, I've been invited on numerous talk shows to give performances, so I throw myself into work.

I was steamrolled into that performance with Brad Baker. I felt uncomfortable with how he tried to make our performance seem more amorous than it should have been.

And it's annoying how the media keeps trying to make a thing of us. I hardly know the guy. He did ask me out on a date, but I promptly turned him down. My heart can't bear the thought of getting close to anyone but Erik.

I suppose I should let that go since Erik made it clear that I've served my purpose and he doesn't want me anymore. All he wanted was someone to perform his music for the world to hear.

I'm not sorry I did it. I'm not sorry for sleeping with him or falling in love with him.

And yes, I'm in love with him. I realized that after he sent me away and I couldn't stop thinking about him. He doesn't want me anymore, but I can't just turn my feelings off.

So, when the host of today's show asks me a personal question, I answer honestly.

"So, Miss Young, you've wowed the world with your voice. First, in a video your friends posted of you singing karaoke and most recently performing one of the elusive Erik Duvall's compositions. But tell us. How's your love life? Are you in love with anyone?"

"Yes," I answer with a soft smile as I think of Erik. I'm not going to put him on the spot by mentioning his name on the air, but if he's watching this, maybe he'll get my subliminal message.

"Oh!" The talk show host's eyebrows raise into his hairline. "Who's the lucky guy? Anyone we know?" He gives me a conspiratorial wink, but I smile and shake my head.

"So, you're not ready to divulge that secret yet?" he presses.

I smile again and look down. Thankfully, he backs off, and the conversation returns to my singing.

———

Erik

My heart falls when I see Harper on the screen answering that yes, she's in love. I might have let her go, but I've watched every interview and performance.

I suppose it's as it should be. It sure didn't take her long to fall in love with Brad. My stomach sours at the thought of his hands and lips on her.

I raise the remote to flip the TV off but find that I

can't. They're doing the open call session where people can call in and give their thoughts on the day's show. Everyone who calls in is speculating on who Harper's in love with.

One caller catches my attention. Her name is Chrissy, and she claims she's a waitress at the diner where Harper used to work.

"Oh, yes, we're close friends, and she's in love with Brad. I mean, we talk every day."

My mouth presses into a firm line. Well, that does it then. It looks like it is Brad. One of her close friends has just confirmed it. I wasn't aware she had any particularly close friends, but why would this girl lie?

I feel like someone has taken a knife to my stomach. Part of me is telling myself to stop being pathetic, get up off this couch and go after my woman. I claimed her first. She's mine.

Yet there's that other part of me that's telling me that I did the right thing, that she doesn't belong to me, doesn't deserve to be chained to a monster like me, someone who can't even leave the shadows when she deserves to be in the light.

God knows I've been miserable every day since I let her go.

I take another sip of my brandy. I've never been

much of a drinker, but I've drank more since Harper left me than I ever have.

It doesn't help. It doesn't matter how drunk I get, the pain doesn't go away.

Still, I'm dying without her. I get drunker and drunker, wallowing in my self-pity. At the height of my drunkenness, I grab my phone and fire off a text, wishing her happiness with Brad. It's the least I can do. I'm her music teacher. I should be glad for her success, and I should want her happiness—even if it's not with me.

After I send the text, I stare into my cup morosely. I'd gladly go through the pain of having my face sliced up again if it meant I wouldn't have this soul-deep ache over losing her.

The only thing that will help is being buried deep inside her, looking into her eyes, and feeling that soul-deep connection with her—a connection I've never had with anyone but her.

So what if it was all a farce? So what if she doesn't love me? She gave herself to me, didn't she? She told me she was mine.

I clench my jaw. Why am I sitting here trying to be all noble when I'm anything but. Brad motherfucking Baker can have any woman he wants on the face of the planet, but I can only have one. I only want one.

Harper Young.

I leave the rest of my drink sitting untouched on the table as I get up to go take a shower.

It's time for me to take back what's mine.

Harper

I GET Erik's text right before I'm set to perform.

My eyes bug out of my head. What? He thinks I'm in love with Brad? Why in the world would he believe that?

But then I think back about how I admitted I was in love but didn't specify who, and the media *has* been shipping Brad and me together.

Oh, my God. Is that why Erik let me go? Did he believe all that stuff the media put out that first night? Did he think I wanted to sing a duet with Brad? Did he think I'd had a secret fling with Brad or something?

While part of me knows I should be angry at his

assumptions, especially after I gave *him* my virginity and slept in his bed for days before my debut, my heart breaks because I know the insecurities behind his thoughts.

He thinks I want Brad and not him. My heart clenches painfully even as hope flutters to life in my chest.

What if he still wants me but sent me away because he thought I didn't want him?

I straighten my back with resolve. I'm going to make it clear once and for all who I'm in love with.

I'm going to put it all on the line and pray that Erik accepts my offer. There's only one way I know to prove how serious I am about him.

As I walk out onto the stage, a hush falls over the crowd. I hold the microphone up to my lips, but before the orchestra cues up, I begin to speak.

"There's something I want to say to everyone before I perform tonight."

If possible, the crowd grows even more silent because this is entirely unprecedented. I don't care if the producers get mad at me for going off-script. This has to be said.

"There's been a lot of speculation about who I'm in love with. I'm going to say his name here and now so everyone knows."

I take a deep breath, praying that Erik is watching and that he loves me. "The man I love is my teacher, Erik Duvall. Erik, if you're watching this, I love you with my whole heart. I love you like I've never loved anyone, and I can only hope you feel the same way. If you do, please meet me at Times Square tonight. I'll be waiting there at midnight, and I hope you show up."

I lower the microphone before I lift it again to add, "And I also hope you know that every time I sing, it's only for you." I glance over at the orchestra and nod. "I'm ready now, and this song is for the man I love. Erik Duvall."

Applause sounds throughout the studio as the opening strings of my song begin.

I sing, imagining that it's Erik I'm singing to. Even though I'm in a room full of people, it's Erik's beautiful face I see in front of me. I see him sitting at the piano, his fingers flying over the keys. I see him looking up at me, his eyes dark and intense as he sings with me. My body hums as I remember how he took me on that same piano.

I sing with my whole heart and soul to Erik and only Erik. My voice soars higher and clearer than ever before. I know it does because when the last strains of my song die away, people leap to their feet, cheering and clapping louder than any performance I've given.

I give a little bow. I want to hurry and get out of here and go wait for Erik. I only pray that he can overcome his fears enough to show up. I overcame mine to confess to the world that I love him. He can reject me in front of everyone, and while that will be embarrassing as hell, it won't compare to the heartbreak of losing him.

After the performance is over, I walk off the stage with shaky legs. I don't bother to change out of my dress before I have a taxi take me over to Times Square.

I swear half of the people at the studio followed me over here because a huge crowd is gathered to see if my lover shows up.

My face is flaming as I stand in the middle of the circle and try to keep my wits about me. I hear soft murmurs all around me. I know what everyone's asking. Is he coming? Is she going to be stood up?

I have the same questions, only I go one further. Did I ask too much of him? Maybe he does love me, but I've pushed him too soon. Maybe I shouldn't have asked him to come out in front of all these people. Maybe this is just too much, too soon for him.

The clock gets closer and closer to midnight, and I start getting more and more nervous that he's not going to come.

When it's one minute away from midnight, my shoulders slump as reality comes crashing in on me.

He's not going to come. I asked too much of him. I know he's insecure about his scars and doesn't want to show them to the world. Why did I think he would leave the comfort and safety of his home for me?

He doesn't want me after all. I've misread everything, but at least he knows how I feel. I won't have to spend the rest of my life wondering what would have happened if only I'd been brave enough to tell him. Even though I'm going to walk out of here looking like an idiot, I don't regret it.

I see the pity and sympathy in everyone's eyes as I turn and slowly walk away. The crowd parts to let me pass, but then murmurs ripple through the gathering and I hear my name being called in that beautiful voice, a voice I feared I'd never hear again.

"Harper!"

I turn, my heart beating erratically in my chest.

"Harper!" he calls again.

My eyes widen, and my heart jumps with joy when I see Erik pushing his way through the crowd. His tall, muscular form races toward me, and he looks just as handsome as ever—scars and all.

He grabs my hands when he reaches me, his eyes

searching mine, chest heaving. "Did you mean what you said, sweetheart?"

I can't speak, so I nod at him, tears stinging my eyes. "But it's okay if you don't—"

He doesn't give me the chance to finish that sentence before his lips crash down on mine.

Applause explodes around us, but I barely register it. All I can think about is his arms wrapping around me and pulling me flush against him.

"I love you too, my little songbird," he whispers against my lips before he pulls back and looks down at me with adoration. "I worship the ground you walk on. I've been in misery without you."

I don't ask him why he let me go. It's inconsequential. None of it matters now. All that matters is that we're together

"Holy shit!" I hear someone say. "It's Erik Duvall!"

"Hey, Mr. Duvall!" someone else calls out. "Do you plan on sharing any more of your compositions?"

Erik looks surprised that people are speaking to him normally. Someone else asks him where he learned to compose the way he does. Another asks where he gets his inspiration and how long it takes him to complete a piece.

No one asks about his scars, and I'm grateful to these people for restoring his faith in humanity.

Erik becomes more comfortable as he realizes no one's going to hound him about his scars because they're more interested in his music.

He clasps my hand in his and holds me right next to him as he answers their questions.

"Do you sing, Mr. Duvall?"

"Yes." A hidden smile plays at the corners of his lips, and I flush, wondering if he's remembering us singing together. The heated look he gives me when he glances my way lets me know that he is.

"Will you sing publicly now?" someone else asks.

"Possibly, but only if Harper will sing with me."

I'm grinning from ear to ear as I look up at him.

"How about you two sing a duet?" someone suggests.

Erik looks down at me with a raised eyebrow. "Now, there's an idea." He winks at me, and my cheeks flush.

People begin peppering us with more questions, wanting details about our romance. When the questions become too invasive, Erik politely tells the crowd that it's time he takes me home. He handles everything so well that you'd never know that he hasn't been in the spotlight his whole life.

There are hoots and hollers and whistles, and I couldn't be happier.

"Thank you," Erik tells me as he leads me away from the crowd and over to where Jenkins is waiting for us.

"For what?" I ask as he slides us into the backseat.

"For bringing me out of the darkness and into the light." He lifts my hands to his lips and kisses them. "For loving me. For singing only for me." His voice breaks on that last bit, and I cup his face and press my lips against his.

"I'll always sing only for you," I tell him honestly.

"Then let me get you home, my little songbird, where I'll make your body sing only for me too."

He kisses me again, and my soul sings.

EPILOGUE

Four Years Later

Erik

MY WIFE'S voice melds with mine as we sing one of my newest compositions together on stage. Her eyes are locked on mine, and we might as well be alone because she's the only one I see when we're singing together like this.

Just wait until I get her backstage. I already feel myself hardening at just the thought, but I try to keep myself somewhat under control so I'm not standing here with a boner in front of this live audience. I swear, as soon as we get back in that dressing room, I'm going to ravish her. If the way her pretty cheeks flush is any indication, she reads the promise clear as day in my eyes. Fuck, I bet she's already soaking wet.

We have two children, Christian and Megara, but I'm always pushing for a third. I love nothing more than seeing my wife's belly round with my child so all the world can see that she's good and bred, that she's *mine*.

Harper is my life. She *saved* my life. She brought me out of the darkness and showed me that not everyone focuses on my appearance. Yes, a few have asked about my scars, but Harper made me realize that it's not always with malicious intent when they ask. It's just curiosity.

I don't rehash the particulars of the war. I merely mention that I got my scars in the line of service, and people seem to respect that, some going so far as to call me a hero. I wouldn't call myself a hero, but I wear my scars with pride now, seeing them the way Harper does, as a testament to my service and character.

I have the courage to come out in the world and do so many things now, and it's all thanks to Harper. My love, my life, my wife. Just *mine*.

Our voices collide together in a crescendo of sound. As we finish the song, applause takes over, and people leap to their feet, chanting for an encore.

They're sure as hell not going to get more tonight. I can't wait another moment to be inside my wife.

I grab her hand and pull her from the stage, practically dragging her back to our dressing room. When we get to the door, I lift her into my arms and carry her over the threshold just like I did when we were first married

I slam the door behind us with my foot and then spin her and press her up against the hard wood. Her lips are turned up, waiting for mine to descend. She's as hot for me as I am for her, and fuck if that doesn't make my blood boil even hotter. Thank god she's wearing a dress because I make short work of pulling it up and ripping the flimsy little panties straight off her body. I'll buy her another pair.

I free my aching length from my pants and thrust into her as her legs wrap around my waist. We both growl in unison as I slide into her hard and deep, just the way she likes it.

"You drive me crazy when you look into my eyes and sing like that. Had me hard for you up there on stage in front of all those people. You like that too, don't you, my dirty little girl?" I grit in her ear. "You like making me hard in front of everyone so the entire world can see how much I want you."

"Oh god!" she moans.

"You say my name whenever you're writhing on my dick," I reprimand her.

"Erik!" she amends.

"That's a good girl," I praise her, and she practically purrs. She loves it when I talk filthy to her and praise her.

"You getting ready to let that body sing for me now?"

"Uh, huh," she moans.

My balls draw up tighter than a bowstring, and I know I can't hold back any longer. I rock into her quickly, our bodies creating the most beautiful symphony, more beautiful than anything I could have ever written on my own.

She screams my name as she falls apart on me just as I let go and roar out my release. I fill her until she's overflowing, my sticky release dripping between our legs.

I carry her over to the couch and set her gently on it before I kneel in front of her and lay my head on her lap.

"I love you, my little songbird," I tell her reverently before I lay a kiss on her inner thigh, silently thanking whatever deity is out there for giving me this precious girl.

"I love you too, Erik," she tells me as she strokes her finger over my scarred face.

I turn my face into her hand and press a worshipful kiss against her palm.

I no longer feel like half a man or a beast.

With Harper, I'm whole.

THE END

Read the rest of the Heart of a Wounded Hero series: www.heartofawoundedhero.com

Want more books by Emma Bray? See her website for a complete list of all her books: www.authoremma bray.com.